TREASURY OF FAIRY TALES™

# SLEEPING BEAUTY

Illustrated by Katherine Lawless

Modern Publishing
A Division of Unisystems, Inc.
New York, New York 10022

Once, long ago, there lived a king and queen, whose only wish was to have a child. When, at last, the queen gave birth to a beautiful baby girl, the king was so overjoyed that he decided to hold a big celebration.

Seven of the fairies in the kingdom were invited to the celebration, and each bestowed a magical gift on the royal child.

"She shall be the most beautiful princess in the world," said the first fairy.

The second fairy promised her charm and kindness, the third promised that she would dance as gracefully as an angel, the fourth said that she would sing like a nightingale, the fifth gave the gift of laughter, and the sixth promised her love.

Suddenly, another fairy burst into the palace! She
had not been invited to the happy occasion, and was
angry. Old and crabby, this fairy rarely came out of the
dark tower in the deep woods where she lived. Everyone
had forgotten about her.

"It is now my turn to bestow a gift on your daughter," she cackled. "When the princess is sixteen, she will prick her finger on a spinning wheel and die!"

The wicked fairy then vanished from the palace. The king and queen were horrified.

The seventh and youngest fairy, who had not yet made her wish for the princess, stepped forward.

"My magical power is not strong enough to undo the spell of an older fairy," she said. "But I can change it. The princess will not die when she pricks her finger. Instead, she will fall into a deep sleep which will last for a hundred years until a handsome prince will awaken her."

The king wanted to protect his young daughter. He ordered that all the spinning wheels in the kingdom be collected and destroyed in a great fire.

The princess grew more beautiful each day. As time passed, everyone forgot the evil fairy's spell.

One afternoon, the princess wandered about the palace, exploring every corner and passageway. A steep flight of stairs led her to a little room at the top of a tower.

There she found a little old woman hunched over a spinning wheel. It was the evil fairy in disguise.

"Whatever are you doing?" asked the princess.

"Spinning flax into thread, my dear. Would you like to try?" asked the old woman.

"Oh, yes!" said the princess. But the moment she began to spin, she pricked her finger and fell into a deep sleep!

"At last!" exclaimed the evil fairy, pleased that her long-ago curse had fallen upon the princess.

The king and queen were heartbroken to discover their beautiful daughter in a deathlike sleep. The king gently placed the princess on a soft bed where she would sleep for one hundred years.

The youngest fairy, hearing the sad news, cast a spell over the entire palace, causing everyone inside to fall asleep.

"Time will stand still, and no one will grow older," the fairy said. "When the princess awakens, she will not find herself alone."

As the years passed, a thick, thorny hedge grew up around the palace—so tall that only the highest towers could be seen from afar.

A hundred years later, a handsome prince, while out riding, saw the palace towers peeping above the hedge in the distance.

"Is that a palace?" he asked the local people.

No one seemed to know. But one old man remembered hearing about a beautiful princess who had fallen under a spiteful fairy's spell.

The prince vowed to rescue the princess.

Leaving his horse behind, the prince drew his sword and began to hack his way through the dense thicket.

Struggling with all his might, the prince swung his sword, cutting through the thorny branches.

Suddenly the enchanted palace stood before him.

When the prince entered the palace, he saw sleeping knights, ladies, and servants. The king and queen were slumped motionless on their thrones, their heads bowed sadly.

The prince searched the castle until he came upon a steep flight of stairs. He followed the stairs to the little room at the top of the tower.

There, on a bed of silk and satin, lay the loveliest maiden the prince had ever seen!

He was so enchanted by her beauty that he could not help bending forward and kissing her.

Instantly, the princess awoke. The evil spell was broken.

Hand in hand, they hurried down the tower steps to the throne room.

The entire palace came back to life. The king and queen awoke and embraced the happy couple. The knights, the ladies, and the servants all cheered. And outside the palace, the hedge magically disappeared.

The prince and princess were married the very next day.